School for
Ghosts Girls

Don't miss any of the haunted

adventures at Boo La La!

#1: School for Ghost Girls

#2: Spooktacular!

Boo La La

School for Ghosts Girls

Ghost Girls RULE!

By Rebecca Gómez

Illustrated by Monique Dong

SCHOLASTIC INC.

As ever, for Nelson.

ISBN 978-0-545-91798-8

10 9 8 7 6 5 4 3 2   16 17 18 19 20

Printed in the U.S.A.   40
First printing, September 2016
Book design by Lizzy Yoder

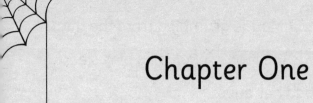

Chapter One

Gong! Gong! Gong!

"Oh my goodness!" CJ cried. She sat up in her bed and pushed the hair out of her eyes. "I'd forgotten how loud the alarm gong is!"

It was the first day of the new school year at Boo Academy, the School for Ghost Girls (affectionately referred to as Boo La La). The ghost girls were in their dorm room in Coffin Hall.

"It sounds like it's right outside our door!" Tiny complained from the next bed. She sat up and twisted around. She preferred sleeping with her feet on her pillow and her head where her feet belonged. Being a basketball-player-sized ghost wasn't always easy!

Gong! Gong! Gong!

"We're up!" Maude grumbled from the third bed in the room. She took off her frilly pink sleep mask and rubbed her eyes.

"I was dreaming that it was still summer vacation," she said. "But I'm glad that we're all back at school." She looked around sleepily. "I think we did a good job decorating last night!"

Tiny and CJ followed her gaze. In their new room, three twin beds were lined up in front of large windows, and three identical dressers faced

the beds. The black ceiling paint was flaking off in patches and the gray stone walls had lots of beautiful cracks. Lovely cobwebs hung in every corner. Their door, like every door in the dormitory, had a large banner saying GHOST GIRLS RULE! Their room was perfectly gloomy.

Tiny had hung three posters of her favorite basketball player, Caspera Jones, above her bed. Maude's purse collection was neatly lined up on a bookshelf. CJ's stuffed bat perched on her headboard.

Still lying in bed, Tiny said, "I can't believe we're finally back! It was a long summer without you guys!"

CJ nodded. "I'm happy that we're back together, but I'm afraid third grade is going to be so hard!" she said. "I heard that Mrs. Graves is a really tough teacher. I am not looking forward to her

7

Undead Language Arts class! I mean, how much work can she expect us to do? Someone told me that last year her class had to write a paper that was four pages long! And they didn't even get to choose their own topic—"

"CJ," Maude interrupted. "Don't worry! We're together again and we're going to have a great year!"

Maude, CJ, and Tiny had been best friends since almost their first day as preschool ghosts.

Now it was the first day of third grade. Maude headed to the closet to pick out her first-day-of-school-outfit. As she looked, she tried—and failed—to stifle a huge yawn.

"What should I wear?" she muttered. "It's so important to make a good impression." Maude was very fashion-forward.

"We're already impressed with you, Maude!" Tiny said. "If anyone, Ms. Finley is the one to wow!"

"Piece of cake," Maude said confidently.

Ms. Finley was Coffin Hall's new dorm mother. Coffin Hall was nestled next to the cemetery, just inside the gates of Boo Academy. Where humans saw only open parkland, any ghost could see the old redbrick buildings surrounding a grassy courtyard. Classroom buildings and dormitories were tucked under huge, dark, ancient trees. The school's cemetery was perfect for haunting practice.

Yesterday, the school's ancient, battered, and enormous school bus had traveled to airports, train stations, and bus terminals to collect students coming from quiet villages, frantic cities, and everywhere in between. Ghost girls came from far and wide to attend Boo Academy.

When that bus had pulled down the gravel driveway to the school, a beaming Ms. Finley had been waiting for the third graders in the academy's cavernous entry hall. She'd worn a white shirt and a long black skirt, and her graying hair had been pulled back in a messy bun. Her glasses had thick black frames with a pattern of scattered white skeleton bones. She knew each third grader's name and gave each girl a big hug as she got off the bus.

"I like Ms. Finley so far," CJ said. "But why did we need a new dorm mother again?"

"I know why," Maude said. She usually did. "Last year, Miss Glider was caught passing out Halloween candy to human children. So of course she was asked to leave the school, because even kindergarten ghosts know the first rule of ghosting: No direct contact with humans!"

Tiny shuddered.

"After all," Maude continued, "how could Miss Glider help us be the best ghosts we can be if she breaks that rule? Imagine if humans learned that Boo Academy existed! It would be horrible."

"I don't want to think about it!" CJ said.

"Don't worry. I heard that Ms. Finley is a Boo La La girl herself, so she'll know the rules," Maude told them confidently.

"You're probably right," said CJ. "At least I hope you are! What do you think they'll serve for breakfast? What if Lucinda sits next to me at lunch? Do you think she's still upset that I outscored her on the Levitation final last year?"

"CJ!" Maude and Tiny said together.

"Oops!" CJ said. "I'm sorry! You know that when I get nervous, I can't stop talking!"

"We know," Tiny said. "And we love you anyway!"

"Besides," Maude said, "Lucinda cheated and you still outscored her!"

"I don't know about her cheating," CJ said.

"I know," Maude said firmly. "I saw her using her foot to keep that chair in the air. I don't know how Mr. Vex missed it! You have a real talent for levitation; most adult ghosts can't even do what you do!"

"But you know Lucinda," Tiny added. "No grudge like an endless grudge."

"Are we ready to head down to breakfast?" Maude asked her friends. She had dressed carefully in a new pair of jeans and a colorful top.

"Let's go!" Tiny answered. "I'm starving." As usual, she was wearing basketball shorts and a T-shirt.

"I'm ready," CJ said. "Do you like my shirt?" She was wearing gray pants and a T-shirt that said LEVITATION IS MY THING!

Maude and Tiny laughed. "It's great!" Tiny said.

Maude pulled open their door and they joined the other third-grade girls heading down to the dining hall. But there was a terrible smell in the air!

"Ugh!" Tiny cried. Everyone was plugging their noses.

"What is that horrible stink?" Maude cried. "Can't we open a window somewhere?"

"Excuse me! We're trying to get down to breakfast!" a loud voice called from behind them. It was Lucinda and Helen, who pushed their way past. Lucinda just had to be first in everything.

Maude, Tiny, and CJ looked at one another

and smiled. Apparently, summer hadn't changed Lucinda.

Ms. Finley hurried up behind them, a warm smile on her face. Today, her glasses were red, with tiny BOOS scattered all over them.

"Good morning, girls!" she cried. "I'm so happy to see that you all heard the morning bell! Of course, I'll wake you up if you ever miss it, but it's good to be independent as soon as possible!"

"Oh my gosh, Ms. Finley!" Maude said, waving her hand in front of her nose. "What is that smell?"

"What smell?" Ms. Finley asked.

Lucinda pushed Maude to the side and complained. "It's cruel to make young ghosts suffer like this. Everyone knows our noses are especially sensitive!"

"I need some fresh air!" CJ said. "This is really bad. I mean, what could be making such a

bad smell? You don't think there's a fire, do you? What if it *is* a fire? Where are the fire exits? We forgot to talk about them last night—"

Tiny tapped CJ on the shoulder and shook her head.

"Stop talking and save your oxygen," she whispered with a smile.

"Achoo!" Ms. Finley sneezed.

"Boo!" her students answered, because that's what polite ghosts do.

"Thank you, girls. I'm sorry, I don't smell anything. But if it's bothering you all so much, let's hurry down to breakfast!" Ms. Finley herded them down the stairs and into the dining room.

Faint gray smoke curled around the exposed beams on the dining-room ceiling.

"Why is there smoke?" CJ asked in alarm.

Now Ms. Finley looked concerned. Principal Von Howl glided toward them across the empty dining room, beaming. His black suit was rumpled and stained, and his stovepipe hat perched jauntily on the side of his head.

"Good morning, girls," he boomed.

"Good morning, Principal Von Howl," the students answered.

"Unfortunately, as you can tell, there was a kitchen incident this morning," he explained. "Cook Eerie forgot a vat of porridge on the stove, and the whole pot burned. It's a shame, because she made her special porridge for your first breakfast. But there are plenty of other good things to eat."

He led them out to the dim, gloomy entry hall, where the long wooden dining-room tables and chairs had been moved. They were already starting to be filled by girls in other grades. At the back, several tables groaned under the weight of the food spread out on top. Gentle steam wafted up from stacks of pancakes and waffles. Fresh fruit was piled in giant bowls, and pitchers of juice stood next to boxes of cereal. High above it all, brown bats swooped and darted through the air.

"Does it smell better out here?" Ms. Finley asked, and the girls nodded.

"How can she not notice the smell?" CJ whispered to Maude as they walked over to the food. "I thought even adult ghosts had a great sense of smell."

"I have no idea!" Maude answered. That was unusual for Maude.

Tweet! Tweet!

A loud whistle startled the girls. It was Mrs. Von Howl, Boo La La's gym teacher and dining-room monitor. She was the principal's wife, and she was little but very strong. While Principal Von Howl was known for being strict but fair, Mrs. Von Howl was mostly just known for being strict. She always wore her whistle around her neck, and seemed to use it as often in the dining room as on the playing field.

"Dig in, girls!" Mrs. Von Howl urged them. "Time waits for no ghost!"

"I see Mrs. Von Howl is still whistle-happy," Maude whispered to her friends.

CJ surveyed the spread. "Yummy! Pirate Bones cereal, my favorite!" she said.

"I'm trying the pancakes," Maude decided.

"I think I'll have both," Tiny announced.

They heard Lucinda's voice behind them. "Hurry up, Helen! We have to get to the food before Tiny does, otherwise there might be nothing left!"

19

As Lucinda and Helen pushed past them,
Maude growled, "That's not very nice!"

Tiny sighed. "It's okay, Maude, just let it go."

"There's plenty of food for all of us," CJ said
staunchly, glaring at Lucinda and Helen.

Lucinda just stuck out her tongue.

"Oh, that's mature," Maude noted. Tiny and CJ giggled.

They all finished getting their food and sat down. Except for the strange smell, their first morning of third grade at Boo Academy was off to a great start!

Chapter Two

The soft squeaking of the bats was the loudest sound in the entry hall as the hungry ghosts settled down to eat breakfast.

Gong! Gong! Gong!

Principal Von Howl led the girls into the auditorium for the welcome assembly. As was Boo La La tradition, the assembly started with the Pledge of Haunting. The ghost girls recited the familiar words with their arms crossed on their chests, right hand on left shoulder, left hand on right shoulder:

It is my duty, stated intention, and

greatest wish to be the

best ghost I can be.

I solemnly swear to haunt

to the very best of my abilities

at all times and in all places.

"Now, ladies," Principal Von Howl said from
the stage, "before we take our seats, which school
is the best school?"

"Boo La La!" shouted sixty girls in unison.

"Thank you. You may be seated," the principal told them as he took off his hat and placed it on
the podium. "Welcome to the start of Boo Academy's
1,358th school year! We know it's going to be an
exceptional year for each one of you."

He gave a big smile, then abruptly became
more serious. "There are just a few administrative
issues that I'd like to bring to your attention. As you
know, fitness equipment is to remain in the gym.
We cannot have a repeat of last year's disaster,
when chains were borrowed and never returned.

We understand that you want to practice rattling outside of the classroom, but you must be responsible for the items you've borrowed. The grounds crew was finding chains all over the campus, all summer long! Now, if I could turn your attention to the code of conduct . . ."

As Principal Von Howl continued his careful description of appropriate and inappropriate behavior, Maude's mind started to wander. She was confident that she knew the rules of Boo La La even better than the principal.

Glancing to her left, she saw Ms. Finley at the end of their row, paying rapt attention to Principal Von Howl. She had one leg crossed over the other, and peeking out from below her long skirt was the tip of what looked like . . . a scuffed brown shoe!

Maude did a double take. Then she rubbed her eyes. A shoe?! She'd only ever seen shoes in pictures of humans. Ghosts didn't wear shoes! They didn't need to; they simply glided. Besides, shoes would keep you from passing through walls. That was just basic haunting!

"Look at Ms. Finley's foot!" Maude whispered to CJ, who was sitting on her right.

CJ glanced over toward the end of the row, then she, too, did a double take. "What is that?"

25

"I think it's a shoe!" Maude said. "I've never seen one in real life."

"What are you guys whispering about?" Tiny leaned over to ask.

"I can't be sure," Maude answered. "But it looks like Ms. Finley is wearing shoes!"

Tiny's eyes grew wide. "Why would she do that?" she whispered frantically.

"Would you please be quiet? Some of us are trying to listen!" Lucinda, sitting in the row ahead of them, turned around and hissed. She said it just loudly enough for Ms. Finley to hear.

Ms. Finley looked from Lucinda's angry face to Maude, Tiny, and CJ and, with a secret wink at them, put one finger up to her lips.

The three friends dutifully turned back to the stage, where Principal Von Howl was still talking. "And now, I ask you to give your complete attention to Mrs. Von Howl, your gym teacher. It's time to talk about Field Day!"

Everyone cheered. Field Day was an annual event that kicked off the school year. The whole school was divided into six teams, with students from all grades on each team. Every team had two teachers as coaches.

"I hope my team colors work with the clothes I brought," Maude muttered.

Mrs. Von Howl floated up to the front of the stage and blew her coach's whistle. She was frowning.

"Good morning, ladies!" she said.

"Good morning, Mrs. Von Howl," the students echoed back.

"Field Day is this Friday, starting at ten a.m. sharp," she began. "Team assignments are posted by the door. When you have a chance to look at the team rosters, I think you'll agree that I've done a good job of making up equally matched teams. There will be the usual games and contests: gliding races, egg tosses, a tug-of-war, an ectoplasm balloon battle, and, finally, our annual student-versus-faculty basketball game," Mrs. Von Howl said.

At the words *basketball game,* Tiny felt both very excited and very nervous.

Mrs. Von Howl continued. "The winning team will receive homework passes for an entire day—"

At this, the students burst out in cheers. But they were quickly silenced by Mrs. Von Howl's whistle and glare.

"And most important," she went on, "the victorious team will have bragging rights until next year's Field Day. I, therefore, urge you to take Friday's contest very seriously." With that, she floated off the stage.

"Thank you, Mrs. Von Howl," the principal said as he went back to his podium. "I'm sure we'll have a fabulous day. As always, we will be kind and respectful to one another. Win or lose, we will be good sports. We each have different gifts, and one ghost's strange is another ghost's normal. We'll all try our best, won't we, girls?"

Maude, CJ, and Tiny, along with all of their schoolmates, clapped and cheered.

"One more time, girls!" Principal Von Howl called above the noise. "Which school is the best school?"

"Boo La La!" shouted the students.

Chapter Three

All sixty ghost girls began filing out of the auditorium.

"How's your game?" CJ asked Tiny. "Any chance of us beating the teachers this year?"

"I hope so," Tiny answered. "I worked out a lot this summer! But we need to start talking strategy."

"You're right—I need a strategy to survive Field Day!" Maude laughed.

"You'll do fine," Tiny reassured her friend. But they all knew that Tiny would be the real star. Her first love was basketball, and she practiced all the time. Maude's talent, however, was not athletic— while all three girls were great students (how else would they have been admitted to Boo La La?), Maude was the ghost at the top of their class.

"I'm in good shape for the races, though," Maude told them. "I practiced floating drills all summer!"

Finally, they reached the team roster lists. Maude, CJ, and Tiny were on the same team! They high-fived and cheered, "Boo La La!"

Next to them, Lucinda asked Ms. Finley if she would be playing in the student-faculty basketball game.

"Most definitely, Lucinda," Ms. Finley said. "My hook shot may not be too accurate, but I'm very enthusiastic!"

"We're going to win this year, I know it!" Tiny whispered. "But not because Ms. Finley is playing for the other team," she added hastily.

"Oh, girls, you're all winners!" said Ms. Finley, overhearing Tiny. Tiny grinned back at her.

After they'd passed Ms. Finley, Lucinda snuck up behind Tiny and hissed, "I wouldn't be so sure of winning, if I were you."

"Yeah," chimed in Helen. "You're not nearly as good as you think you are!"

Tiny just rolled her eyes, but secretly felt a pang of nerves in her tummy.

"Come on, CJ and Tiny," Maude said. "Let's get out our school supplies. I think my dad bought me a new shrieking book!"

With that, they turned their backs on Lucinda's smirk.

The sun shone brightly on Boo Academy, so, naturally, the ghosts had morning recess inside where it was nice and gloomy. CJ, Maude,

and Tiny were sitting together in a cobwebby corner.

"I've been thinking a lot about Ms. Finley," Maude announced to her friends.

"I think she's super!" CJ said.

"I agree," Maude said. "She's very nice, and I certainly appreciate her fashionable eyewear. But she couldn't smell the horrible burned porridge—and she wears shoes!"

"It's very weird," Tiny said.

"I've never, ever met—or even heard of—a shoe-wearing ghost," Maude added. "Something just doesn't add up."

"Don't look at me." Tiny laughed. "Math is not my strong subject!"

"What are you saying, Maude?" CJ asked nervously. "She seems really nice and friendly and helpful! She learned all of our names before we

35

even got here. Didn't you say she's a Boo Academy graduate? She also seems to know that Lucinda is nothing but trouble, and did you see the way she—"

"CJ, you're doing it again!" Tiny said gently.

"Oops! Sorry," CJ answered. "But Maude is making me nervous now."

"I don't mean to scare you, CJ," Maude said. "But this could be very serious. Ghosts have an excellent sense of smell, and Ms. Finley does not. Ghosts don't wear shoes, and Ms. Finley does."

Maude took a deep breath and looked at her friends.

"What if she's not a ghost after all?" she asked. "What if she's a . . . *human*?"

CJ gasped.

Tiny turned even more translucent than usual.

The friends were silent as each thought

about the consequences of a human knowing about Boo Academy. For thousands of years, humans and ghosts had existed side by side. Ghosts were taught, from their earliest years, to protect the divide between the human world and their own. The job of a ghost was simple: provide humans with occasional gentle scares, remind them of someone they knew who had died, or, in some cases, frighten a human out of bad behavior. That's what all their haunting classes taught them. That's what their training prepared them for. Humans were not supposed to know much about ghosts, and definitely nothing about Boo Academy.

Finally, Maude said what they were all thinking—the phrase they'd been taught since they were baby ghosts: "Doubt is good."

Tiny said, "Remember Mr. Vex's lecture last year? We all know how humans are. If they're not sure that we exist, we can haunt all we want. If they can prove that we exist, they'll find a way to get rid of us."

"Humans don't like mysteries!" CJ agreed. "I think they're afraid of a little doubt!"

"We need to test Ms. Finley," Maude said. "For the sake of Boo La La, we need to prove that she's one of us."

Chapter Four

When recess ended, the ghost girls turned their thoughts back to class. "I'm so excited for Supernatural Science!" Tiny cried.

"Me too!" Maude agreed.

"Not me," CJ said glumly. "But I guess it's good to get it over with in the morning. I have a hard time memorizing all those charts and tables. Does ghostly mist rise half an hour *before* or *after* sunset? What's the difference between an aura and an emanation? Why do we need to know all that stuff? We won't really start haunting until we graduate. Oh, and, what if Ms. Finley is a human and ruins everything?"

"Don't worry, CJ," Tiny consoled her friend. "To answer your science questions, ghostly mist rises a half hour *after* sunset. And an aura is an atmosphere or mood, while an emanation is something emitted. Supernatural Science is my favorite class, and I'm pretty good at it."

"Pretty good?" asked Maude. "You're not pretty good; you're fantastic. You're the only one in our grade who received a one hundred on the final last year."

Maude always knew that type of information. Her friends agreed that she could probably accurately calculate any of their classmates' averages within two percent. Maude just liked to know things.

"And don't worry about Ms. Finley, either," she whispered to CJ. "I'll figure out something!"

"Well," CJ said, trying to smile as they floated into class, "at least we have Undead Language Arts to look forward to next period."

"Ugh!" Tiny said. "Please don't get me started on *that* class!"

The three friends looked at one another and even CJ had to giggle. Part of the reason why they got along so well was that each ghost girl had different strengths and weaknesses. Maude was the undisputed leader of the trio. She tried hard not to be bossy, but she was bright and friendly, and the best student shrieker at Boo La La! CJ could be a little bit shy, but she talked nonstop when she was nervous or upset, and she was amazing at levitation. Tiny had always been the tallest girl at Boo La La by more than a head (one that's still attached to a body, that is!). And while most ghosts have no sense of the passage of time, Tiny can tell you, at any moment, exactly what time it is.

"We're going to have a great year together,

no matter what!" Maude said as she opened the classroom door.

They were surprised to see Mr. Vex's huge old desk covered in balloons.

"Good morning, class!" he greeted them.

"Good morning, Mr. Vex," they answered.

"I've got a really fun experiment planned for us today," Mr. Vex continued. "It is designed to help you better understand correct haunting practices and how to harness static electricity to your benefit."

"I know this experiment," Lucinda announced. "We did it at my summer enrichment camp. Do I have to do it *again*?"

"That's great to know, Lucinda!" Mr. Vex told her. "Perhaps you'd be willing to help me instead? You could start by giving each student a balloon and a piece of tissue."

Lucinda puffed up with pride. She walked around the classroom, dispensing the tissues and balloons.

"Everyone got their materials?" Mr. Vex did a quick check of the classroom. "Perfect! Now, who can tell me the most prevalent image humans have for ghosts?"

Maude raised her hand. "They think we look like floating bedsheets with eyeholes cut out!" she said.

"Correct," Mr. Vex told her. "You and I know that we look perfectly normal, but for some reason, humans have a strange idea about our appearance. We will just accept that for the sake of this experiment."

Following his instructions, the students penciled in eyeholes on their tissues. Maude added a smiling mouth and earrings to hers. The girls placed their tissue "ghosts" flat on their desks. They then vigorously rubbed their balloons on their hair to build up a strong charge. When they held the balloons over the thin tissue, each rose up and seemed to dance.

"This is awesome!" Tiny cried.

Mr. Vex allowed the girls about fifteen minutes to play with their "ghosts." Despite the obvious fun her classmates were having, Lucinda decided not to participate. She sat at her desk and looked bored.

"This was actually a twofold lesson," Mr. Vex said as he called their attention back to him. "We've learned about electricity and how it acts on objects, and we've learned a little bit about the difference between our reality and the way humans often perceive us. You may well use this information for your future hauntings!"

"I can feel myself getting smarter!" Tiny whispered to her friends.

"I got a real *charge* out of that experiment!" CJ joked.

Maude groaned, but in the back of her mind, she was thinking about Ms. Finley. Was she an imposter, a human among ghosts, trying to learn all the secrets of the ghost world?

By the time Undead Language Arts and gym class were over, the ghost girls were ready for lunch.

"Wow!" Tiny said as she placed her tray of food on the dining room table. "The day is flying by!"

"You were awesome in gym class, Tiny!" Amy said as she passed behind them. "I wish I was on your Field Day team." She lowered her voice. "Lucinda and Helen are on my team."

"Oooh, sorry to hear that, Amy," Tiny said as Amy took her seat at the next table. She turned to Maude and CJ. "Field Day is just for fun, anyway, right?"

"Correct," Maude said. "But sometimes I think that Lucinda's idea of fun is very different from ours!"

CJ and Tiny nodded, and they all began eating their lunches.

Tiny closed her eyes as she chewed. When she'd finished her mouthful, she grinned at her friends. "I've been dreaming of Cook Eerie's lasagna all summer long!"

"Happy lunching, ladies!" Ms. Finley's cheerful voice came from the end of their table. "After you've eaten, I'll see you outside for recess. It's turned into a lovely gray day and you need to glide around and let off some mist!" She bustled off to get her own lunch. Her skirt was so long that it dragged on the floor, hiding any evidence of shoes.

"She's so nice! She just *can't* be human!" CJ moaned.

Through narrowed eyes, Maude watched her make her way across the room. CJ and Tiny exchanged glances. They knew that look very well. Maude was thinking seriously and deeply about something.

"She *seems* like a ghost . . ." Maude murmured. She had decided: Operation Test Finley would begin that very night!

Chapter Five

After a brisk game of White Ghost/Gray Ghost, the girls headed to their afternoon classes.

"I'm so glad we have Unnatural Numbers after lunch," Maude said. "I'm all fueled up and ready to learn!"

"Maude," Tiny said. "You know I love you, but your insistence on learning all the time may make me lose my appetite!"

The three friends laughed. They knew very well that absolutely nothing could make Tiny miss a meal!

Ms. Raven started speaking as soon as the girls found their seats. "As you know, ladies, third grade is a huge year in Unnatural Numbers. And the first topic we'll be exploring is telling time!"

The whole class groaned, except Tiny.

Ms. Raven just smiled at them. "No worries," she said. "Telling time is extremely difficult for ghosts—"

"Not for Tiny," Maude announced to the class.

Tiny blushed.

"Excellent," Ms. Raven answered. "I'll look forward to your help, Tiny." She beamed at Tiny and continued, "The passage of time is something that doesn't impact our daily lives, but effective haunters must master this skill. Please turn to page 2,406 in your textbook. We're going to pick up right where we left off last year. Let's get right to it!"

The ghost girls were back in their rooms after dinner. Unnatural Numbers class had been followed by Intermediate Haunting.

"I'm so happy that Mr. Clank is teaching Haunting class," CJ said.

"Me too," Tiny said. "He already knows what a great levitator you are, CJ. It was fun when he asked you to demonstrate for the rest of us."

"I think it bothered Lucinda, but it serves her right!" Maude added.

"Thanks, guys," CJ answered. "That's one test I know I'll do well on!"

"Speaking of tests . . ." Maude said.

"We know you love them, Maude!" CJ teased.

"Yes, I do," Maude agreed. "But what I'm thinking is that we need to do some tests to determine if Ms. Finley is really one of us."

Tiny nodded. "That's a good idea. What should the tests be?"

"To create an effective test, we need to think

about the differences between ghosts and humans," Maude said.

"We've already talked about our superior sense of smell," CJ said.

"And the fact that we don't wear shoes," Tiny said.

"And, except for Tiny, most ghosts can't gauge the passage of time," CJ said.

"We don't like very bright lights," Tiny offered.

"We can glide right through humans, but not other ghosts," CJ added.

"We don't like dogs," Maude continued. "Well, except for CJ! For the rest of us, they're much too barky and they try to point us out to humans."

"I like all animals," CJ said.

"We have to knock three times before we enter a room where there are other ghosts," Tiny said. "Oh, and we can pass through walls, but we never do that when we're not haunting. Remember last year, when Lucinda glided through the wall into gym class instead of coming through the door?"

"I do," Maude said. "Mrs. Von Howl was so angry."

"I remember her lecture," CJ said. She mimicked Mrs. Von Howl's voice, " 'Girls, gliding through walls when you're not haunting is *just not done*!' "

Maude giggled, then got serious again. "We'll do some simple tests. If she is truly a ghost, then no harm done. If she's human, on the other hand . . ." Maude hesitated.

"Who knows what might happen?" CJ jumped in. "I mean, humans don't belong at Boo La La. Humans belong on the outside. That's why Boo Academy is camouflaged to them. That's why humans see a grassy park instead of our beautiful school. That's—"

"Exactly, CJ!" Maude said to stop her friend's nervous babbling.

"Sorry," CJ said.

The room was quiet for a few minutes as each girl was lost in thought.

Then Maude snapped her fingers. "I've got one!" she announced. "Let's call Ms. Finley into our room. We'll pretend that we need help with something. If she knocks before she comes in, she's a ghost!"

"That's so simple," CJ said. "Why didn't I think of that?"

"I'll call her," Tiny said. "I'll pretend I have a question about the dining hall."

"Excellent!" Maude cheered. "Go for it!"

"Ms. Finley!" Tiny bellowed. "Ms. Finleeeey!"

A few moments later, they heard Ms. Finley's voice.

"Is someone calling me?" she asked.

"It's me, Tiny," she yelled.

"I'll be right there, dearie," Ms. Finley answered.

The girls were silent as they waited. And then Ms. Finley opened the door and was bustling into their room, wearing a floor-length, shapeless white gown with her hair trailing over one shoulder in a long braid. There was no sign of her glasses.

"What's up, Tiny?" she asked cheerfully.

"Um, I was wondering . . ." Tiny thought quickly. "Do you think Cook Eerie will make pancakes for breakfast again tomorrow?"

Ms. Finley looked surprised, but just nodded. "Yes, I think she will. Is that all?"

"Yes, thank you, Ms. Finley," Tiny answered.

"Okay, then, good night girls," Ms. Finley said, and she headed back to her room.

"Oh, no!" Maude cried when Ms. Finley was gone.

"She didn't knock!" CJ wailed.

"I can't believe this!" Tiny added. "But maybe she just forgot to?"

"Maybe," Maude said.

"I really, really don't want her to be human!" CJ said. "Can't we try again?"

"Should we?" Maude asked.

CJ and Tiny both nodded.

Maude agreed, so they decided that she would call for Ms. Finley. As Tiny had done, she called out loudly. This time, they could hear Ms. Finley's soft footsteps in the hallway.

Knock, knock, knock.

"Come in, please," Maude said.

"Yes, Maude?" Ms. Finley asked.

"Do you know what color our Field Day T-shirts will be?" Maude asked.

"No, I don't," Ms. Finley answered. "But Mrs. Von Howl will tell us soon."

"Okay, thanks, Ms. Finley," Maude said. "Good night."

"Good night, ladies," she answered. "Sweet dreams!"

When she had gone, Tiny looked at Maude. "That was good, right?" she asked. "She knocked, just as a ghost should."

"Hooray for Ms. Finley!" said CJ.

"Guys, I hate to tell you, but we still haven't proven anything," Maude told them. "Ms. Finley knocked one time but didn't knock the other."

"So?" Tiny asked.

"So," Maude said. "That means we still don't know for sure that she's a ghost."

"Now what do we do?" CJ asked.

"Come up with another test, I guess," Maude answered. "Let's sleep on it and talk again tomorrow."

Chapter Six

"Attention, everyone!" Principal Von Howl was making an announcement at breakfast the next morning.

It took several minutes and several more "Attention, everyones!" before the room quieted down.

"Thank you, ladies," Principal Von Howl said. "As you *may* have heard, Field Day is tomorrow! So after breakfast tomorrow, no regular classes will be held."

The dining room erupted with cheers and clapping. Principal Von Howl gave them a few moments, and then continued.

"I trust you've each had a chance to check

out your team assignments . . . and maybe even done a little strategizing with your teammates," he said.

"I think he takes this *way* too seriously," Maude whispered to Tiny and CJ.

"Are you kidding?" Tiny asked her friend incredulously. "I don't think he is serious enough!"

"Shhh!" The girls glanced down the table to see Lucinda glaring at them, her finger held up in front of her mouth. "Do you three ever stop talking?"

"Why would we?" Maude whispered to Tiny and CJ, who smiled back.

"And now, please listen to Mrs. Von Howl, who has an important announcement," Principal Von Howl said.

"It's time to distribute the Field Day T-shirts," Mrs. Von Howl announced. On a table behind her, cardboard boxes were neatly stacked. "I will call up one team at a time."

Maude, CJ, and Tiny waited patiently, finishing up their breakfasts, as she called up the first team and handed out yellow T-shirts.

"Good!" Maude told them. "I was hoping we wouldn't be assigned yellow this year!"

The first team sat down and then the second team trouped up to receive orange T-shirts.

"Excellent," Maude said.

"Let me guess," CJ asked her. "You didn't want orange, either?"

"Correct," Maude answered.

"You do know that we're going to win no matter what color we wear, right?" Tiny asked.

"Oh, I know," Maude assured her friend. "I just prefer a more neutral color."

"What's a neutral color?" Tiny asked. "Isn't a color a color?"

"Oh, Tiny," Maude sighed. "Orange and yellow are just so . . . clashy!"

Then their names were called and they joined their teammates at the front of the room. Maude was very relieved to see Mrs. Von Howl reach into a new cardboard box and pull out light-blue T-shirts.

"Oh, yes," Maude said happily. "I can definitely work with blue!"

As the girls headed back to their rooms after breakfast, chattering and laughing about Field Day, Maude's attention turned, once again, to the problem of Ms. Finley.

She was preoccupied throughout their whole Supernatural Science class. She didn't even laugh at Mr. Vex's emanation jokes.

CJ and Tiny noticed her silence.

"Is anything wrong, Maude?" Tiny asked as they hurried through the hallways to Undead Language Arts.

"Hmmm?" Maude asked.

"Why are you so quiet?" CJ asked. "Are you upset about something? I mean, something besides Ms. Finley? Besides the fact that our whole world may come crashing down? Besides—"

"You said you liked the blue T-shirts, right, Maude?" Tiny interrupted. "What's going on? Mr. Vex always makes you laugh. But you didn't even crack a smile! 'Why did the ghost cross the road? To emanate from the other side!' That one gets me every time!" She couldn't help laughing again.

"What? Oh, yes," Maude assured her friends. "I love the blue; it absolutely works with the rest of my Field Day outfit."

"Well, that's a relief!" Tiny said, rolling her eyes.

Maude playfully stuck out her tongue at her friend. "I'm sorry," she said. "I admit it; in class just now, I wasn't even listening to Mr. Vex and his jokes.

I'm just thinking really hard about another test for Ms. Finley."

"Okay," CJ told her friend. "You worry about the test. Finding out if Ms. Finley is truly a ghost is the most important thing right now. Tiny and I will take extra-careful notes and we'll catch you up later."

"Thanks!" Maude said.

It wasn't until halfway through Undead Language Arts class that a plan began to form. Oddly enough, it was an innocent comment from Mrs. Graves that started an idea germinating in her head.

They'd been discussing their summer reading book, *Frontier Ghost*, and Mrs. Graves called their attention to various sections. They read some aloud and some silently to themselves.

"What do you think life would have been like for a young ghost on the prairie?" Mrs. Graves asked. "How might haunting have been done differently?"

Lucinda waved her hand.

"Yes, Lucinda?" Ms. Graves asked.

"There was no electricity on the prairie, right?" she asked.

"Correct," Ms. Graves answered.

"So ghosts would have been unable to turn lights on and off to alert humans to their presence," Lucinda said.

"Maybe frontier ghosts caused cooking fires to burn higher or lower?" guessed Tiny.

"That's an excellent suggestion, Tiny," Mrs. Graves said.

"That's what I was going to say!" Lucinda complained.

"Can you think of another way to haunt?"
Mrs. Graves asked her.

Lucinda was silent for a moment.

"Well," she said, "maybe they made noises on
the roofs of houses?"

"Yes," Mrs. Graves said. "We know from some
of our oldest ghosts that they did exactly that."

Lucinda smiled smugly.

"Let's go on to the next passage," Mrs. Graves suggested. "Who'd like to read aloud for us?"

"I will," said Lucinda quickly, looking at Maude curiously. It was usually a competition to see who would speak more often in class: Maude or Lucinda.

But Maude was thinking about the word *passage* . . .

By lunchtime, her plan was coming together.

"I think I've got it," Maude whispered to CJ and Tiny over their turkey sandwiches.

"Great!" Tiny cried.

"What's great?" Lucinda asked from farther down the table.

"Uh . . ." Tiny thought quickly. "My sandwich is great!"

"You can be so strange, Tiny," Helen chimed in.

"One ghost's strange is another ghost's normal," CJ answered loftily. It was a saying that Principal Von Howl was fond of repeating. Ms. Finley had started saying it, too. It made the girls like her even more.

"Whatever!" Lucinda said, turning back to her lunch.

"Later," Maude whispered to her friends, winking, and she began talking about her Field Day outfit.

"So what's the plan, Maude?" CJ asked.

The three girls were tucked in their beds. Tiny's feet were resting on her pillow and CJ's stuffed bat was nestled under her arm. Ms. Finley had just knocked three times and then poked her head in to say good night and turn out their light.

"May all your dreams be scary!" she called as she headed to her room. "Rest up—tomorrow's a big day!"

Maude had insisted that they wait a few minutes to talk about the plan.

"I don't want Ms. Finley to hear us," she cautioned. "I really like her and don't want her to think that we doubt her."

"But we *do* doubt her," CJ pointed out. "Even though I hope she's really a ghost. I don't want her to be human. That would be the worst thing ever!"

"But we have to do what's right for Boo La La," Tiny interrupted. "Right?"

"Right. We all really like Ms. Finley," Maude said. "But to be here, she needs to be a ghost."

The girls lay quietly in their beds and listened as their end of the hallway grew silent.

"Now will you tell us?" CJ asked.

"Yes!" Maude said. "This was a tricky test to come up with—I thought the door-knocking test would work."

"So did we," CJ said loyally.

"But it didn't prove anything one way or another," Maude reminded them. "We talked about a lot of things that are specific to ghosts, but I kept coming back to one fact: Ghosts can pass through humans, but they can't pass through other ghosts."

"That's one of the first things we learn in kindergarten!" CJ said.

"Otherwise, kindergartners would do nothing but stub their toes and bang their heads on each other," Tiny said cheerfully.

"Exactly," Maude said. "So my plan involves one of us trying to pass through Ms. Finley."

CJ shivered. She heard Mrs. Von Howl's voice in her head: *Girls, it's just not done!*

"I know it goes against everything we've been taught," Maude continued. "But if we can pass through her, then we'll know Ms. Finley is human and not a ghost at all. If we can't, then we can assume that she is a ghost and rightfully belongs with us here at Boo Academy."

"So who's going to try?" CJ asked. "And when?"

"Tiny, I think you're our best hope," Maude said.

"Me?" Tiny squeaked.

"You," Maude said. "And tomorrow's our best chance. You're our star basketball player. You're going to be on the court the entire time during the student-faculty game. At some point, you can run right into Ms. Finley."

After a few moments, Tiny answered. "Okay. I'll do it. You guys know how clumsy I can be—my mom always says that my brain hasn't caught up with my body! So it won't seem strange if I bump into her."

"And then either way, we'll know," Maude said. "If you bounce off Ms. Finley, she's a ghost. If you pass through her, she's . . . not."

"Oh, it will be so embarrassing if she's really a ghost!" CJ said.

"But we need to do it," Tiny said, nodding "A little embarrassment will be okay if it means saving Boo La La!"

"Hug huddle!" Maude whispered.

As the three friends embraced, they quietly chanted, "Ghost girls rule!"

Chapter Seven

The girls woke the next morning to absolutely perfect Field Day weather. It was cool, foggy, and raining lightly.

"It doesn't get much better than this!" CJ said.

"I'm just sorry the basketball game is in the gym," Tiny said. "I love playing in the rain!"

"Oooh!" Maude said. "Do I hear thunder? This day just keeps getting nicer!"

Suddenly, Tiny moaned. "Uh-oh!"

"What's wrong?" Maude and CJ asked together.

"I just remembered what I have to do today," Tiny answered. "I'm not looking forward to it!"

"You'll be fine, Tiny," CJ told her friend.

"But what if I mess up?" Tiny fretted.

"You won't," Maude soothed. "I wouldn't have asked you if I didn't know you could do this. The whole thing will be over before you know it!"

"I hope so," Tiny said. "And I hope Ms. Finley is a ghost!"

Maude tried to change the subject. "How do you like my outfit?" she asked. "I wasn't sure about the blue shirt with my red shorts, but I think it works. Do you?"

"You look good, Maude!" CJ said. "I wonder what Ms. Finley's glasses will be like today."

"Oh," groaned Tiny. "Can we please not talk about Ms. Finley?"

"We're all in this together, Tiny," Maude said. "You're the one actually trying to pass through Ms. Finley, but we'll be there to support you. Don't worry about a thing!"

"Ghost girls rule!" the three friends chanted, high-fived, and then headed down to breakfast, where they found Ms. Finley already seated at the faculty table. Her glasses did not disappoint. In honor of Field Day, they sported multicolored stripes and had a #1 on the nosepiece.

"I guess she's feeling pretty confident," Maude noted with a smile as she looked around the dining room. It was a sea of colored T-shirts. The three friends quickly grabbed breakfast sandwiches and juice and joined a noisy group of ghost girls in blue shirts.

"How are you feeling, Tiny?" several of the other girls asked.

Tiny answered them all politely, but her stomach was full of butterflies. She wished the basketball game came at the beginning of the day, not the end. She was going to have to wait through all the other events before she'd get to play.

When everyone glided outside to begin Field Day, Tiny decided to distract herself by making up cheers for her teammates.

Fortunately, Tiny had a lot to cheer about. The day's first event was the long-distance gliding race. It was the race Maude had been practicing for all summer. She and one member from each of the other teams jostled to line up at the race's start. When Mrs. Von Howl shrieked, they were off!

The race required the girls to glide around the entire perimeter of the Boo La La campus. It was a very long distance, so Maude paced herself. She didn't worry when first Amy and then Louise passed her.

She heard Tiny's voice from far away cheer, "Go, Maude!" which made her smile.

Maude kept true to her pace and stayed within striking distance of the leaders. She concentrated on keeping her glides smooth and efficient.

"Keep it up, Maude!" Even among all the cheering, Maude could make out CJ's screams.

Almost before she knew it, the finish line was visible in the distance. Suddenly, someone came gliding on her right. "I'm going to beat you!" Helen huffed as she tried to pass.

Maude knew she had to make her move. Using her last bit of energy, she forced herself to glide even faster and began to edge up on Amy and Louise, leaving Helen behind. With the finish line just yards in front of her, she managed to pull ahead and cross first! She glided right into the arms of CJ and Tiny, huffing and puffing but very happy.

"Way to go, Maude!" Her teammates thumped her on the back and shook her hand.

Maude smiled and slowly glided around in small circles, trying to stay loose and relaxed. When Helen glided by, a scowl on her face, Maude said, "Good race, Helen!"

Helen said nothing.

Next it was CJ's turn to participate in the ectoplasm balloon battle. As every ghost knows, ectoplasm is the material left behind after a successful haunting. Every year, teachers at Boo La La collected it from classrooms, the cemetery, and laboratories . . . everywhere the students practiced. For Field Day, they'd filled colorful balloons with the slippery material.

"I don't understand why you like this game, CJ," Maude said.

"It's so much fun!" CJ answered. "We get to run around the entire school and pelt one another with balloons. It's a blast!"

"If you say so." Maude sighed.

Each participant grabbed two filled balloons. They were allowed to come back to base and pick up more balloons as the contest went on. The winner was the ghost who could go the longest without being "plasmed." Mrs. Von Howl allowed time for the players to scatter around the campus, and then she shrieked to get them started.

The air was immediately filled with the sounds of ghosts shrieking, teammates cheering, and the *splat, splat, splat* as one ghost after another was hit and disqualified.

Nearly all of the balloons had been taken when CJ was finally hit.

"Darn it!" CJ said as she joined her friends, wiping ectoplasm from her T-shirt. "I was sure I could outlast them all!"

"You did really well, CJ!" Tiny comforted her. "You were one of the last ghosts playing."

"But I don't know if I earned any points for our team!" CJ worried.

"Don't worry one bit, CJ," Maude assured her. "The basketball game is still ahead of us and we have the best player at Boo Academy on our team!"

Tiny grinned weakly. The butterflies in her stomach seemed to have turned into angry ravens!

But then it was time for the tug-of-war. A long rope was stretched out on the field. Two teams lined up on one end and two teams lined up on the other. Maude, CJ, and Tiny were at the front of their line, facing Lucinda and Helen and their teammates.

"You're going to lose!" Lucinda called.

"Oh, no we're not!" CJ called back.

At Mrs. Von Howl's shriek, the ghosts started pulling. At first it seemed that Maude, CJ, and Tiny's

84

side would win, but then slowly, inch by inch, Lucinda's side turned the tide.

"Come on, guys!" Lucinda called to her teammates. "Let's crush them! One, two, three, pull!"

And with a mighty yank, Maude, CJ, Tiny, and their teammates were pulled over the halfway line.

"We won! We won!" Helen cried.

Helen stalked over to the three friends. "Sorry, losers," she said, and went back to join her celebrating teammates.

"What happened to being good sports?" Tiny wondered. Maude and CJ just shook their heads and rubbed their sore hands.

Chapter Eight

At lunch, it took the girls a few minutes to realize what was different about Ms. Finley. Her long gray hair was twisted up into its usual bun but, instead of her familiar floor-length skirt and plain top, she was wearing baggy sweatpants and an ancient Boo Academy T-shirt. Dirty lace-up sneakers were just visible under her sweatpants

"Eat up, girls!" she urged them. "You'll need lots of energy this afternoon!"

"Those are definitely sneakers," Maude murmured to her friends.

"She just *can't* be human," CJ groaned. "She's far too nice!"

The dining room grew quiet as the whole school tucked into soup, sandwiches, and fruit. As they ate, Mrs. Von Howl strode to the front of the room to review the events held already and each team's score.

As she had thought, Mrs. Von Howl had done a good job of creating evenly matched teams. By the end of the day, all six teams were within a few points of one another.

Finally, it was basketball game time. One combined student team would face off against the teachers. As the tallest girl at school, Tiny was playing center, her favorite position. She started the game facing Mrs. Graves. To her left, playing point guard, Lucinda was jumping in place to keep limber. Tiny decided to try to make the best of working with her unpleasant teammate.

Tiny windmilled her arms around her head, trying to loosen them up, and attempted to tune out all the noise in the gym. After all, in addition to trying to lead her team to victory, she had another more important job to do. She had to pick the right moment to try to pass through Ms. Finley.

The whistle blew, and they were off. Tiny scored first with a beautiful jump shot. Ms. Finley caught the rebound, scurried down the court, and lobbed the ball. *Clank!* The ball bounced off the hoop.

"Watch your shots," Mrs. Graves called. "No more bricks!"

"Doing my best!" Ms. Finley answered, giving her teammate a thumbs-up.

"Go, team!" Lucinda called. Tiny looked at her, amazed. Lucinda had a determined look on her face—she was totally into the game.

As Tiny sat on the bench at halftime, someone tapped her shoulder. She turned to see Maude just behind her, a worried look on her face.

"You haven't forgotten our plan, right?" Maude dropped her voice to a whisper.

"No," Tiny whispered back. "I guess I'd better find my moment soon?"

"I think so," Maude told her friend. "You got this!" she called as she clambered back up to her seat in the bleachers.

"Huddle up!" Tiny shouted to her teammates. "We can do this," she told them. "We need to hold them off and grab every scoring opportunity! Keep boxing them out, but play clean. Hands in!" she called. Each girl put a hand into the center of the circle, stacked on Tiny's hand at the bottom. "Go, Boo!" Tiny called.

"Boo La La!" the girls all cried as they lifted their hands into the air.

They were nearly to the fourth quarter
before Tiny saw her chance. She'd been very busy
watching Ms. Finley, who actually had an awesome
hook shot. Finally, they were alone running down
the court, Ms. Finley dribbling furiously. Tiny
sprinted up behind her and, taking a deep breath,
put on a burst of speed and headed directly toward
Ms. Finley's back.

"Watch out!" she heard Mrs. Von Howl cry.

The next thing she knew, Tiny was on the floor, looking up at the bright lights of the gymnasium.

"Are you okay?" Ms. Finley's worried face appeared to be floating above her.

"What happened?" Tiny asked, confused.

"You ran right into Ms. Finley," Mrs. Von Howl said. "You bounced back about four feet!"

"I'm so sorry," Ms. Finley said. "I guess I shouldn't have stopped short like that!"

"Nonsense," Mrs. Von Howl said. "We're playing a game of basketball here! Tiny should have watched where she was going!"

A huge smile split Tiny's face. She sat up and searched the crowded bleachers for Maude and CJ. They were both sitting up, beaming at her. Maude was giving her two thumbs-up.

She'd done it! She'd tried her best to pass through Ms. Finley and had miserably failed. She couldn't be happier! Ms. Finley couldn't be a human!

Mrs. Von Howl was looking at her strangely.

"I apologize, Ms. Finley," said Tiny, carefully wiping the giant smile from her face. "I hope you weren't hurt."

"Not at all, dear," Ms. Finley said, straightening her glasses on her face. "I'm made of tougher stuff than that!"

"If you're sure," Mrs. Von Howl said, "perhaps we can finish up this game?"

"Sure thing!" Tiny said happily.

"Let's go!" Ms. Finley agreed.

When the final whistle blew, the score was 72–60, with victory going to the student team. Despite her tumble, Tiny was the leading scorer with thirty-two points.

As quickly as she could, Tiny found Maude and CJ.

"Did you see that?" she asked.

"We sure did," Maude answered.

"You bounced back like Ms. Finley was a trampoline!" CJ said.

"There's absolutely no doubt she's a ghost!" Maude assured them.

"You played very well, Tiny," Lucinda said, coming up behind them. "Thanks for helping us beat the teachers."

Tiny was shocked at Lucinda's kind words. Where was the Lucinda who never missed a chance to say something mean? Who loved to be the center of attention?

"Um, thanks, Lucinda," Tiny answered. "You were pretty good yourself." And she was surprised to realize that she meant it. Lucinda had been a good teammate. She'd followed Tiny's suggestions on the court and had even scored a few baskets. Was it possible Lucinda wasn't so bad all the time?

Maude quickly jumped in. "Well, you all worked together," she said. "Boo La La!"

Chapter Nine

Back in the dining hall that evening, sixty hungry ghost girls wolfed down the traditional Field Day celebration dinner: pizza. Lots and lots of nice cold pizza!

"I am so hungry!" Tiny said.

"Me too," said CJ.

"And you didn't even play in the game, CJ," Lucinda butted in. She was passing by the three friends, her dining tray piled high with pizza.

"Good point, Lucinda," CJ said sweetly. "Guess I'm just a growing ghost!"

Lucinda scowled and took her seat at the next table.

"It seems Lucinda is still Lucinda," Tiny muttered.

CJ and Maude just nodded back at her, their mouths full of pizza.

Principal Von Howl stood up at the faculty table. "Who's ready for ice cream?" he called.

"We are!" everyone screamed. (Except for Maude—she didn't like ice cream.)

"Thanks to the dining room staff, there's a make-your-own-sundae bar in the kitchen. Please help yourselves!" Principal Von Howl urged. "While you're scooping, we'll be tallying the Field Day results."

"I hope we won!" CJ said as they walked into the kitchen.

"Me too," Tiny answered. "But even if the blue team didn't win, I'm happy that the students won the basketball game!"

When the girls were done scooping ice cream, ladling fudge sauce, and squirting whipped cream, they all trouped back to the dining room. Maude's bowl was filled with nothing but whipped cream and fudge sauce.

"Yummy," she said.

"That's such a strange sundae," Tiny said.

"One ghost's strange is another ghost's normal!" The three friends laughed together.

Soon Mr. Von Howl was standing at the front of the room again. "I have the final tally," he announced. "But first, Mrs. Von Howl is going to make one presentation."

"You all played, glided, and threw very well today, girls. I'm extremely proud of you!" Mrs. Von Howl began. "In particular, one student stood out for her efforts on the basketball court."

Everyone immediately looked at Tiny, who blushed and looked down at the table.

"The faculty and I are recognizing Tiny as the basketball game's Most Valuable Player."

"Hooray, Tiny!" Maude shouted.

"Tiny! Tiny! Tiny!" the other students chanted, banging their spoons on the wooden table.

Principal Von Howl allowed them a few

moments to celebrate, then called them to order again.

"As MVP, Tiny's team is awarded extra points," he began. "All six teams were very close in points, but Tiny's recognition puts the blue team ahead."

"We won!" Maude cried. "Hooray for Tiny!"

"Go, Blue!" shouted CJ.

"Congratulations, blue team!" Principal Von Howl said.

Tiny called her nine teammates over and lead them all in a cheer. *"Boo La La! Blue La La!"*

After a few minutes, Ms. Finley came over to them. "Come along, girls," she said. "You've all had a long day and must be exhausted."

The third graders cleared their places and followed her out of the dining room.

"Well done, all of you!" she said as they reached their hallway. "I am so proud of each of

my girls. You brought honor to Coffin Hall. And congratulations to the third-grade members of the
blue team!"

"Thank you, Ms. Finley," the girls said as they
disappeared, in groups of three, into their rooms.

"What a relief!" CJ cried as soon as they
were alone in their room.

"Wait a minute, we can't go to bed yet,"
Maude announced.

Tiny groaned. "I'm so tired! Aren't you?"

"Yes, I am, but we need to speak to Ms.
Finley first," Maude answered darkly. "I have just a
few unanswered questions."

"Really?" CJ asked nervously. "Aren't you
satisfied? Ms. Finley can't be human, right? Didn't
Tiny prove that on the basketball court? I was so

scared, but now I feel much better. I love Ms. Finley, and I'm so happy she's a ghost—"

"We need to ask her about a few things," Maude interrupted. "It will all be okay. Come on, let's get this over with."

Reluctantly, CJ and Tiny followed Maude to Ms. Finley's room.

"Come in," she called when Maude knocked on her door.

She was not yet in bed, but she was dressed in her white nightgown, with her hair in its long braid. On her feet were fuzzy gray socks.

"Hello, ladies," she said. "I hope everything is okay!"

"Um, yes, Ms. Finley," Maude began.

She looked at CJ and Tiny, but they had no idea what to say.

"Achoo!" Ms. Finley cried.

"Boo!" said Maude, CJ, and Tiny.

"You are such polite ghosts!" Ms. Finley said. "Please excuse me, I just need to grab a tissue."

As she hurried into her bathroom, CJ and Tiny looked at Maude. What were they doing here? What should they say?

Ms. Finley came back, wiping at her nose with a tissue.

"This cold is driving me crazy!" she said. "It was bad enough sneezing nonstop, but now my nose won't stop running. I just don't know what to do!"

"You have a cold?" Maude asked.

"Yes," Ms. Finley said, "a real doozy!"

"Does it keep you from smelling?" Maude asked.

"Why, yes, it certainly does!" Ms. Finley said. "It's been just beastly."

"Is that why you couldn't smell the burned

porridge our first morning here?" CJ asked, catching on to Maude's line of questioning.

"What? Oh, yes," Ms. Finley said. "I couldn't smell anything for days! And, as you know, not having a powerful sense of smell is a very unusual situation for a ghost!"

"Yes," Tiny said. "We know!"

"But you girls didn't come to hear about my health." She laughed.

"Well, um," Maude said, "we . . . we have a question for you."

"Yes?" Ms. Finley asked.

"Why do you wear shoes?" Tiny blurted out.

"What?" Ms. Finley asked.

Maude, feeling bolder now, said, "We noticed that you wear shoes."

"None of us have ever seen a ghost wearing shoes. But you do," CJ added.

"Yes, I do," Ms. Finley said. "You might not be able to guess now," she explained. "But when I was here as a student at Boo La La, I was quite the athlete."

"You were?" Tiny asked.

"Oh, yes." Ms. Finley laughed. "I won a number of first-place ribbons in my day. Unfortunately, I may have run a little too much as a young ghost. Now my feet give me all sorts of trouble. The doctors said I should wear my shoes whenever possible."

Maude, CJ, and Tiny were astonished.

Ms. Finley continued, "It took me a while to get used to them. After all, what ghost wears shoes? Not many of us, I can tell you that. I have to special order them! But I do find that when I wear my shoes, my feet feel much better."

"But how do you pass through walls?" Maude wanted to know. "Don't your shoes stop you?"

"Of course," Ms. Finley said. "So I take them off before I pass through anything."

"Just like that?" Maude asked.

"Just like that," Ms. Finley said firmly. "Now, is there anything else you're curious about?" she asked.

CJ and Tiny looked at Maude. She answered for them all, "No, Ms. Finley."

"Excellent," Ms. Finley said briskly. "Then I suggest we all turn in for the night. You three must be exhausted after today's events. I know I am!"

"Good idea," Maude agreed. "This has been a very busy week."

"Yes," Ms. Finley said. "I hope you girls are enjoying Boo Academy. It's a wonderful, precious place to be."

"Yes, Ms. Finley," the girls answered together.

"Very well, then," Ms. Finley said. "I'm

delighted to know that you're settling in so nicely. I know that we're going to have a *spooktacular* year together!"

Maude, CJ, and Tiny laughed, and knew that she was absolutely right. They were together again, their new dorm mother was definitely a ghost—a funny and kind one—and their team was the Field Day champion. They couldn't wait to see what Boo La La had in store for them next!

Read on for a sneak peek at Maude, CJ, and Tiny's

next adventure at

Spooktacular!

"I stayed up way too late last night," Maude whispered to her friends. "If you two hadn't woken me this morning, I definitely would have slept through breakfast!"

"Why did you stay up so late?" Tiny asked.

"I just couldn't put down *A Complete Behind the Scenes Guide to Boo La La*. It's fascinating!" Maude answered.

"Can I see the book again?" Tiny asked.

"Sure," Maude answered, as she eased it gently out of her bag.

"It's so old!" CJ exclaimed.

"It is very old," Maude agreed. "Just like Boo Academy. And there's so much great information inside!"

Tiny started leafing through the pages. "Hmmm," she said. "I just see a bunch of charts and floor plans. I'm not sure what you're so excited about, Maude."

"Hey! What's that?" CJ asked, pointing at folded piece of paper peeking out near the back of the book. "That page is not the same color as the rest of the book."

"I don't know," Maude answered, using two fingers to pluck out the paper. "It fell out last night when I was finally going to sleep. I just stuck it back in anywhere."

She smoothed out the paper on the table in front of them. It was a hand-drawn map! BOO ACADEMY was written in spidery script at the top of the page. Maude recognized a few of the school's current buildings. There was a compass rose in the lower-right corner. And in the upper-left corner there was an X drawn above the words MY TREASURE.

"What?!" Maude cried in astonishment.

"It's a treasure map!" Tiny said, her eyes wide.

Don't miss any of the
Dolphin
❧ School ❦
books!

#1: Pearl's Ocean Magic

#2: Echo's Lucky Charm

#3: Splash's Secret Friend

#4: Flip's Surprise Talent

#5: Echo's New Pet

#6: Pearl's Perfect Gift